TEC

TEC

I've Been Burping in the Classroom

in the

Classroom

And Other Silly Sing-Along Songs

Burp!

Created by
Bruce Lansky

Illustrated by
Stephen Carpenter

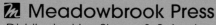
Meadowbrook Press
Distributed by Simon & Schuster
New York

Contents

Welcome Back to School

(sing to the tune of "My Bonnie")

"Dear students, the summer has ended.
The school year at last has begun.
But this year is totally different.
I promise we'll only have fun.

Chorus
"Sit back. Relax.
The school year is gonna be fun, so fun.
We'll play all day.
The school year is gonna be fun.

"We won't study any mathematics,
and recess will last all day long.
Instead of the Pledge of Allegiance,
we'll belt out a rock 'n' roll song.

"We'll only play games in the classroom.
You're welcome to bring in your toys.
It's okay to run in the hallways.
It's great if you make lots of noise.

Chorus

"Your video games are your homework.
You'll have to watch lots of TV.
For field trips we'll go to the movies
and get lots of candy for free.

"The lunchroom will only serve chocolate
and Triple-Fudge Sundaes Supreme."
Yes, that's what I heard from my teacher
before I woke up from my dream.

Kenn Nesbitt

3

Do You Get Marked Down?

(sing to the tune of "Do Your Ears Hang Low?")

Do you get marked down
when you're acting like a clown?
Do you make your teacher mad?
Do you make your teacher frown?
Do you try to get attention,
but instead you get detention?
Do you get marked down?

Do your eyes roll back
when you have a nap attack?
Is your body still awake,
but your mind has hit the sack?
Are you tapped upon the shoulder
when you're drooling on your folder?
Do your eyes roll back?

Do you do your best
to prepare for every test?
Are you pinning Post-It notes
to the pocket of your vest?
Do they reassign the seating
every time they catch you cheating?
Do you do your best?

Linda Knaus

Do Your Big Feet Smell?

(sing to the tune of "Do Your Ears Hang Low?")

Do your big feet smell?
Do your dirty socks as well?
When you're playing with your friends
here's a certain way to tell:
If they're pointing at your sneaker
and you see they're getting weaker,
then your big feet smell.

Is your breath so vile
when you yawn or burp or smile?
When you look from side to side,
have the kids all left your aisle?
Are your classmates almost dying?
Is the teacher really crying?
Then your breath is vile.

Steve Charney

My Locker
Is Obscene
(sing to the tune of "America:
My Country 'Tis of Thee")

My locker is obscene—
worst place you've ever seen.
It's such a mess.
Place where old math tests lie,
old lunch, old apple pie.
The janitor will surely die
when I leave in June.

I'll clean it right away.
I'll throw this stuff away,
like ham and cheese,
bologna green with mold,
thick milk that's four months old,
five chocolate bars I never sold.
I should clean this soon.

I'll start with last month's fruit,
my First Communion suit
from second grade,
three coats, four pairs of shoes,
eight books I'll never use,
pink globs of gum with two more chews,
and an old balloon.

I'm almost halfway through.
Don't know just what to do
with all these ants.
They're crawling everywhere.
Millions are here, I swear.
They're even in old underwear
that I lost last fall.

I think I'm almost done.
I'm sure there's only one
more pile to go.
Five T-shirts almost clean,
my bag from Halloween,
and finally one jellybean.
Whew! I've done it all!

Kathy Kenney-Marshall

Lovely Teacher

(sing to the tune of "Clementine")

Lovely teacher, lovely teacher—
eyes of periwinkle blue.
You are such a pretty creature,
and I'm so in love with you.

How I long for your attention,
so I'm acting like a fool.
Put me down for some detention,
just don't send me home from school.

Oh, I'm filled with pain and sorrow,
for my teacher is so cute,
but she won't be here tomorrow,
'cause she's just a substitute.

Linda Knaus

Angelica the Beautiful

(sing to the tune of "America the Beautiful")

Angelica's so beautiful,
her teeth are pearly white.
And when she smiles, I turn to mush.
She's such a stunning sight.

It's true I have a crush on her,
of that there is no doubt.
That's why I tease her every day—
so no one will find out.

One day when we walked home from school,
she slipped her hand in mine.
I thought that she was sending me
a clear romantic sign.

I smiled and gave her cheek a kiss
to prove my love was true.
That's when she gave my face a slap,
so now it's black-and-blue.

Bruce Lansky

9

Mystery Meal
(sing to the tune of "The Old Gray Mare")

Great green globs of
greasy, grimy gopher guts,
mutilated monkey meat,
little birdies' dirty feet.
Hot school lunches
aren't fit for kids to eat.
So pass the ketchup, please.

Pizza topped with
rotten eggs and sauerkraut,
seven-week-old speckled trout.
Toss it at your friends and shout.
Start a food fight—
you'll get caught, without a doubt.
So pass the pepper, please.

Adapted by Bruce Lansky

The Battle Hymn of the Repulsive

(sing to the tune of "The Battle Hymn of the Republic")

Mine eyes have seen the kitchen,
which is why I bring my lunch.
I have smelled the things they're cooking,
and they're toxic, I've a hunch.
And the salads are so soggy that
you'll never hear a crunch.
I bring my lunch to school!

Chorus
I can't stand the food they serve me!
I can't stand the food they serve me!
I can't stand the food they serve me!
I bring my lunch to school!

They torture nose and taste buds
with both hamburger and spuds.
There are meatballs in a gravy that's
like iridescent mud.
Mashed potatoes hit both tray and stomach
with a sick'ning thud.
I bring my lunch to school!

Chorus

It's amazin' when a raisin
starts to crawl across your cake;
that was when I first decided
the dessert was a mistake.
And I wouldn't like to guess what's
floating in that chocolate shake.
I bring my lunch to school!

Chorus

Michael Bowman

Oh My Darling, Valentine

(sing to the tune of "Clementine")

In a toy store
on a Sunday
with a dollar forty-nine,
I need something,
just a dumb thing,
for my brand-new
valentine.

Oh my darling,
oh my darling,
oh my darling,
valentine.
I'm uneasy,
kind of queasy,
but you're still my
valentine.

Yes, it happened
in the classroom
when you said,
"Will you be mine?"
I was muddled
and befuddled,
so I answered,
"Yeah, that's fine."

Then you called me
in the lunchroom.
You had saved a
place in line.
And I knew that
it was true that
I was now your
valentine.

I went shopping
for a present,
and I saw this
blinking sign:
"Here's a pleasant
little present
for a brand-new
valentine."

So I bought it,
and I brought it
in my backpack
right at nine.
Do you like it?
It's a spy kit
with a flashlight
you can shine.

I could tell you
didn't like it
when you said I
was a swine.
How exciting!
I'm delighting.
I have no more
valentine.

Till another
person stopped me,
and she asked,
"Will you be mine?"
This is crushing!
Oh, I'm blushing.
I've another
valentine.

Kenn Nesbitt

I've Been Burping in the Classroom

(sing to the tune of "I've Been Working on the Railroad")

I've been burping in the classroom
since I ate my lunch.
We had beefy, cheesy tacos,
and I gobbled down a bunch.
Can't you hear my belly rumble,
full of greasy taco meat?
Can't you hear the girls all whining,
"Your breath smells like your feet!"

Tacos taste so swell,
but they make you smell.
It's those spicy beans and me-e-eat!
When you eat a bunch
of that zesty lunch
for sure you won't smell sweet.

Someone needs to tell the lady
when she cooks our lunch today-ay-ay
please leave out the grease and spices
so we can go out and play.

Kathy Kenney-Marshall

14

The Kindergarten Concert

(sing to the tune of "America the Beautiful")

The kindergarten concert was an interesting show.
When Peter walked onto the stage, he yelled, "I have to go!"
Poor Katie was embarrassed, but she had nowhere to hide.
She raised her dress to hide her face. Her mother almost died.

They sang their song while Wyatt burped, and then he did a dance.
Then Michael fell while spinning 'round, and Peter wet his pants.
The music teacher at the end said, "There, I'm glad that's done."
The kindergarten bowed and said, "Let's sing another one!"

Robert Pottle

My Favorite Fibs

(sing to the tune of "My Favorite Things")

Spot ate my homework; he thought it was chicken.
Aliens landed and gave me a lickin'.
Can't raise my hand; I got poked in the ribs.
These are a few of my favorite fibs.

Can't wear a backpack; it's bad for my shoulders.
Can't find my notebooks and can't find my folders.
Can't write in pen; I'm allergic to ink.
Can't change for gym 'cause the uniforms stink.

Chorus
When I'm flunking,
when I'm tardy,
when the due date's passed,
I simply remember my favorite fibs,
and then I am free—at last!

I wasn't running, just super-fast walking.
Got laryngitis; can't do any talking.
Last weekend's party was wrecked by my twin.
Can't eat school lunch 'cause I want to stay thin.

Book-eating creatures broke into my locker.
Twisted my ankle; good riddance to soccer.
Don't have a note 'cause my doctor was sick.
Sometimes I find an excuse that will stick.

Chorus

Neal Levin

It's Finally Friday

(sing to the tune of "Miss Suzy")

It's Friday, and I'm so glad.
It's been a crazy week.
I got chewed out on Monday.
Since then it's all been bleak.

I lost my lunch on Tuesday.
A parent went insane,
which shocked me so completely,
I almost popped a vein.

I poked my eye on Wednesday.
The nurse gave me a shot.
She sent me to the doctor
for fainting on the spot.

On Thursday I was tardy.
I kinda overslept.
The snack that I was craving
was stolen in a theft.

And so it's finally Friday.
No pencils and no books.
No sitting in detention.
No teachers' dirty looks.

By Friday I'm exhausted—
no energy or breath.
That's the day you'll hear me shout,
"Rejoice, TGIF!"

And twice a month on Friday,
I know just why I stay:
I'm the school's new principal—
that's when I get my pay.

Paul Orshoski

My Teacher Loves Her iPod

(sing to the tune of "Miss Suzy")

My teacher loves her iPod.
It's always in her ear.
She doesn't mind it if we joke
or chat 'cause she can't hear.

If we don't pay attention,
she doesn't seem to care.
Whenever she has music on,
she wears a distant stare.

Our principal dropped by one day,
and she paid no attention.
He took away her iPod
and he sent her to detention.

Bruce Lansky

I've Been Sitting in Detention

(sing to the tune of "I've Been Working on the Railroad")

I've been sitting in detention
since the end of school.
I've been sitting in detention
just because I broke a rule.

Throwing meatballs in the lunchroom
wasn't wise, I fear.
I was aiming at the trash can,
not my teacher's rear.

Teacher let me know
when you'll let me go.
Please don't keep me here all ni-i-ight.
I apologize—
throwing food's not wise.
Don't keep me here all night.

I am going to sneak out of detention
if you will not let me go-o-o-o.
I am going to sneak out of detention,
so, teacher, let me go.

Bruce Lansky

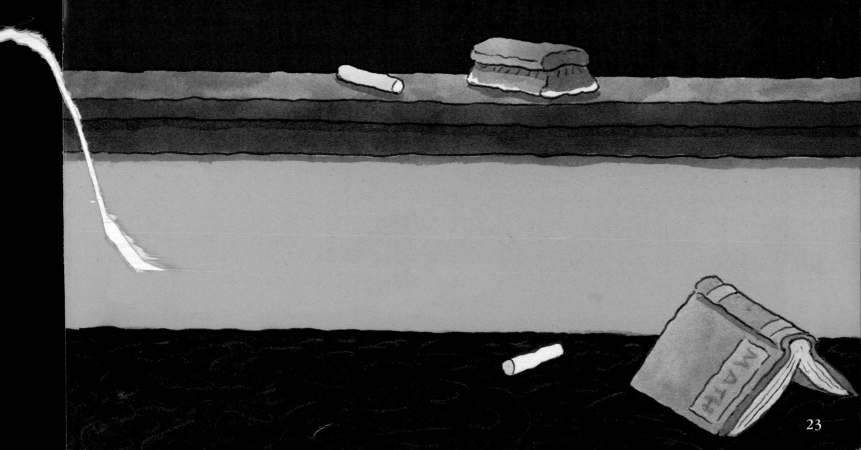

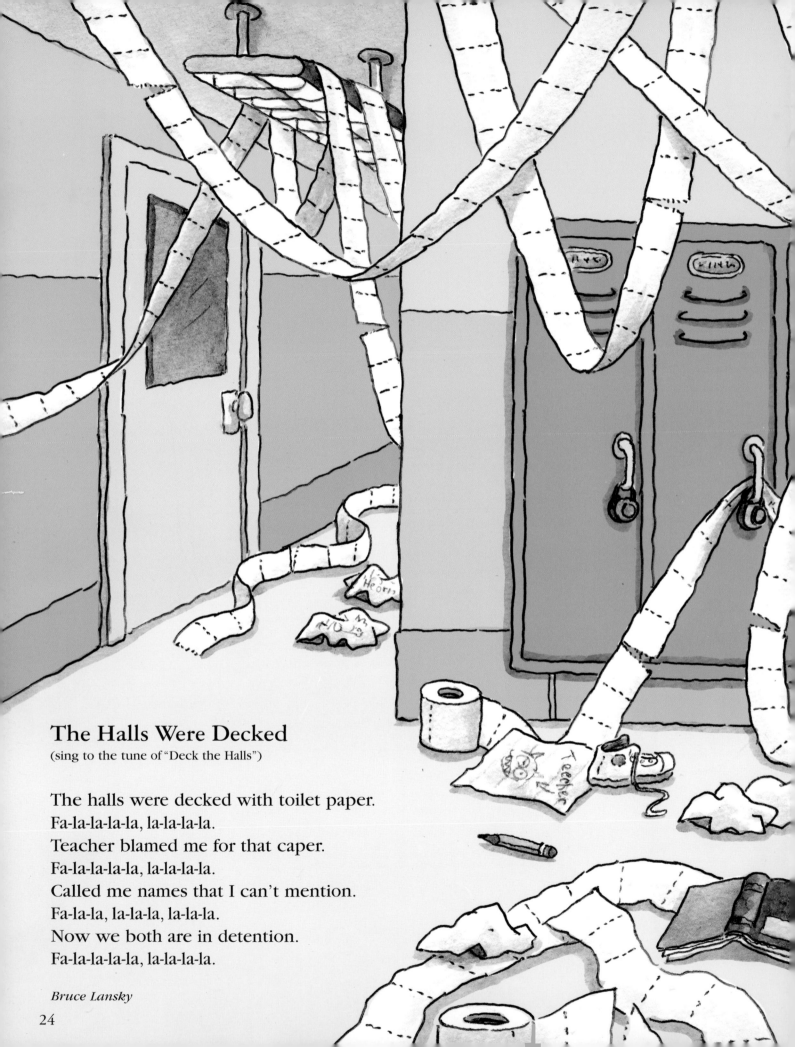

The Halls Were Decked

(sing to the tune of "Deck the Halls")

The halls were decked with toilet paper.
Fa-la-la-la-la, la-la-la-la.
Teacher blamed me for that caper.
Fa-la-la-la-la, la-la-la-la.
Called me names that I can't mention.
Fa-la-la, la-la-la, la-la-la.
Now we both are in detention.
Fa-la-la-la-la, la-la-la-la.

Bruce Lansky

24

I'm a Little Mixed-Up

(sing to the tune of "I'm a Little Teapot")

I'm a little mixed-up. That's a fact.
Coat hooks are empty. Chairs have been stacked.
No one's in the classroom. Something's wrong.
I guess I hid in the john too long.

I'm a little mixed-up. This I know.
Where is my teacher? Where did she go?
When she gave a math test to the class,
I snuck away with a bathroom pass.

I'm a little mixed-up. That's my fate.
Here is my classroom. Here's where I'll wait.
Maybe I was late, but I'm no fool:
On Monday, I'll be the first at school.

Eric Ode

The Teachers Jumped Out of the Windows

(sing to the tune of "My Bonnie")

The teachers jumped out of the windows.
The principal ran for the door.
The nurse and librarian bolted.
They're not coming back anymore.

The counselor, hollering madly,
escaped out the door of the gym.
The coach and custodian shouted
and ran out the door after him.

Chorus
Oh my! Goodbye!
They're not coming back anymore, no more.
How fun! They've run!
They're not coming back anymore.

The lunch ladies threw up their ladles,
then fled from the kitchen in haste,
and all of the students looked puzzled
as staff members scurried and raced.

We'd never seen anything like it.
But still, it was pretty darned cool
to see all the staff so excited
to leave on the last day of school.

Chorus

Kenn Nesbitt

Library of Congress Cataloging-in-Publication Data

I've been burping in the classroom : and other silly sing-along songs / edited by Bruce Lansky ; illustrated by Stephen Carpenter.
   v. cm.
   Summary: Provides silly, school-themed lyrics to popular tunes.
   Contents: The battle hymn of the repulsive / Michael Bowman – Do your big feet smell? / Steve Charney – My locker is obscene ; I've been burping in the classroom / Kathy Kenney-Marshall – Do you get marked down? ; Lovely teacher / Linda Knaus – Angelica the beautiful ; Mystery meal ; My teacher loves her iPod ; I've been sitting in detention ; The halls were decked ; Marching out of school / Bruce Lansky – My favorite fibs / Neal Levin – Oh my darling, valentine ; The teachers jumped out of the windows ; Welcome back to school / Kenn Nesbitt – I'm a little mixed-up / Eric Ode – It's finally Friday / Paul Orshoski – The kindergarten concert / Robert Pottle.
   ISBN 0-88166-521-5 (Meadowbrook Press) ISBN 1-4169-2946-0 (Simon & Schuster)
   1. Children's songs, English–Texts. [1. Schools–Songs and music. 2. Humorous songs. 3. Songs.] I. Lansky, Bruce. II. Carpenter, Stephen, ill.
   PZ8.3.I79595 2007
   [782.42]–dc22

                                    2006007015

Project Director: Bruce Lansky
Coordinating Editor and Copyeditor: Angela Wiechmann
Editorial Assistant and Proofreader: Alicia Ester
Production Manager: Paul Woods
Graphic Design Manager: Tamara Peterson
Illustrations and Cover Art: Stephen & Tad Carpenter

Published by Meadowbrook Press, 5451 Smetana Drive, Minnetonka, Minnesota 55343

www.meadowbrookpress.com

BOOK TRADE DISTRIBUTION by Simon and Schuster, a division of Simon and Schuster, Inc., 1230 Avenue of the Americas, New York, New York 10020

12 11 10 09 08 07   10 9 8 7 6 5 4 3 2 1

Printed in China

Credits

"The Battle Hymn of the Repulsive" copyright © 2007 by Michael Bowman; "Do Your Big Feet Smell?" copyright © 2007 by Steve Charney; "My Locker Is Obscene" and "I've Been Burping in the Classroom" copyright © 2006 by Kathy Kenney-Marshall, previously published in *My Teacher's in Detention*; "Do You Get Marked Down?" copyright © 2007 by Linda Knaus, and "Lovely Teacher" copyright © 2006 by Linda Knaus, previously published in *My Teacher's in Detention*; "Angelica the Beautiful," "Mystery Meal," and "Marching Out of School" copyright © 2007 by Bruce Lansky, and "My Teacher Loves Her iPod," "I've Been Sitting in Detention," and "The Halls Were Decked" copyright © 2006 by Bruce Lansky, previously published in *My Teacher's in Detention*; "My Favorite Fibs" copyright © 2007 by Neal Levin; "Oh My Darling, Valentine," "The Teachers Jumped Out of the Windows," and "Welcome Back to School" copyright © 2007 by Kenn Nesbitt; "I'm a Little Mixed-Up" copyright © 2007 by Eric Ode; "It's Finally Friday" copyright © 2007 by Paul Orshoski, previously published in *My Teacher's in Detention*; and "The Kindergarten Concert" copyright © 2006 by Robert Pottle, previously published in *My Teacher's in Detention*. All songs used by permission of the authors.

Acknowledgments

Many thanks to the following teachers and their students who tested songs for this anthology:

Patti Berger, Groveland Elementary, Minnetonka, MN; Michael Bowman, Robertsville School, Morganville, NJ; Niki Danou, Groveland Elementary, Minnetonka, MN; Jeremy Engebretson, Groveland Elementary, Minnetonka, MN; Kathy Kenney-Marshall, McCarthy Elementary, Framingham, MA; Carol Larson, Rum River Elementary, Andover, MN; Hope Nadeau, East Elementary, New Richmond, WI; Connie Roetzer, East Elementary, New Richmond, WI; and Carleen Tjader, East Elementary, New Richmond, WI.